NICK BUTTERWORTH AND MICK INKPEN

THE MAGPIE'S TALE

Sometimes, grown-ups find it hard to believe in miracles. In Nick Butterworth and Mick Inkpen's delightful *Animal Tales*, special occasions in Jesus' life are seen through the eyes of some of God's smaller creatures, who have no trouble at all understanding exactly what is happening...

Marshall Pickering is an Imprint of
HarperCollins*Religious*
Part of HarperCollins*Publishers*
77-85 Fulham Palace Road, London W6 8JB

First published in Great Britain
in 1988 by Marshall Pickering

This edition published in 1994

Text and illustrations Copyright © 1988
Nick Butterworth and Mick Inkpen

The authors and illustrators each assert the moral right to be
identified as the authors and illustrators of this work

A catalogue record for this book is
available from the British Library

ISBN 0 551 02876-9

Printed and bound in Hong Kong

NICK BUTTERWORTH AND MICK INKPEN

THE MAGPIE'S TALE

JESUS AND ZACCHAEUS

Hello, I'm a magpie. I live in this sycamore tree.

You see the gold ring I'm holding in my beak? I found it. Well, I pinched it really. I used to have lots of stolen things in this nest. Not any more.

Let me tell you the story. It all began yesterday afternoon ...

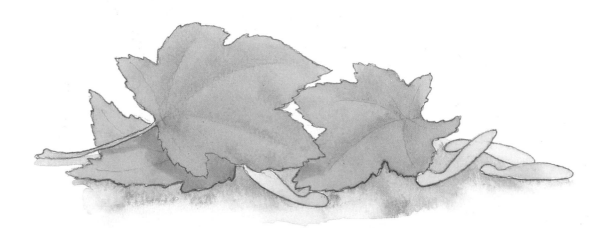

It's a hot day and I'm sitting out of the sun guarding my stolen treasure.

Suddenly I hear the sound of people laughing.

Down below a large crowd is gathering. That's odd. Usually nothing happens around here in the middle of the afternoon.

The people have lined up along the street. They seem to be waiting for someone. I wonder who it is. He must be important.

Look, even Zacchaeus has come out to see. He's the short, fat man who lives in the big house on the corner. Nobody likes him much. He collects the taxes. They say he's a cheat.

Zacchaeus is too short to see over the crowd. He's trying to push his way to the front. But he's too fat to squeeze through, and the people won't let him past.

They're pretending not to notice him at all. Nobody likes Zacchaeus.

Now he's coming over to my tree.
He's climbing up to get a better view!
But his short legs won't reach the
branches. He's puffing and panting and
going red in the face.

Quickly! The important man will be
here soon! Go on Zacchaeus, you can
do it!

Just in time Zacchaeus scrambles into the tree. The crowd starts to cheer and everybody presses forward.

'Hooray, here comes Jesus!'

I can just see his face through the leaves. But who is Jesus? He doesn't look important at all. Not like a King, or a General.

By the look of him he's not even rich. Just an ordinary man.

Jesus walks up to my tree, stops and looks up through the branches. Perhaps he has spotted my treasure sparkling in the sun.

Does he know I stole it? What does he want?

'Zacchaeus, come down,' says Jesus with a laugh. 'I'd like to stay at your house today.'

Zacchaeus nearly falls off his branch. What a surprise. Why would anyone want to stay with Zacchaeus? Nobody likes Zacchaeus.

Zacchaeus climbs down and Jesus
says hello. It's very strange. He speaks
to Zacchaeus like an old friend.

The crowd don't like it at all.

'Why choose Zacchaeus? He's a
cheat and a thief!' says one woman.

Now Zacchaeus speaks out loud, for everyone to hear.

'I'll give half of everything I own away,' he says, 'and everyone I've cheated I'll pay back four times over.'

The people are amazed. What has happened to Zacchaeus? He's like a different man.

Since then I've taken back everything
I stole. The things from my nest have
been turning up all over town!

This golden ring is all that's left. I
pinched it from the big house on the
corner. Zacchaeus left it on the
window sill.

He'll be pleased to get it back,
I should think.

If you enjoyed this *Animal Tale*,
you can also read

The Cat's Tale – Jesus at the Wedding
The Fox's Tale – Jesus is Born
The Mouse's Tale – Jesus and the Storm